# Tame c

Written by Judith McKinnon

Rigby

These animals are
in a pet shop.
People will take
these animals home
and take care of them.
They are tame.

3

These animals don't
live with people.
They live in the jungle
and find food to eat.
They are wild animals.

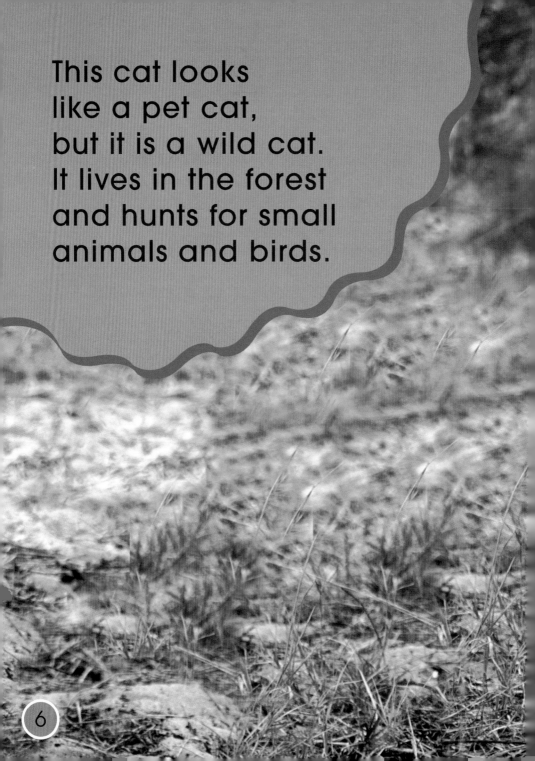

This cat looks
like a pet cat,
but it is a wild cat.
It lives in the forest
and hunts for small
animals and birds.

Iberian lynx

This animal is a wolf.
Some pet dogs look
like this wolf,
but this animal is
a wild animal.
It hunts for its food.

wolf

8

This rat looks
like a pet rat,
but it is wild.
It eats the trash that
people throw away.
Wild rats are not
good pets.

Some rabbits can be tame
and some can be wild.
These rabbits are wild.
They don't live with people.
They live in burrows
with lots of rabbits.

burrow

People take care of their pet animals, but they can help wild animals, too.

# Index

# Guide Notes

---

**Title: Tame and Wild**
**Stage:** Early (3) – Blue

**Genre:** Nonfiction
**Approach:** Guided Reading
**Processes:** Thinking Critically, Exploring Language, Processing Information
**Written and Visual Focus:** Photographs (static images), Index, Labels
**Word Count:** 156

---

## THINKING CRITICALLY
(sample questions)

- Look at the front cover and the title. Ask the children what they know about tame animals and wild animals.
- Look at the title and read it to the children.
- Focus the children's attention on the index. Ask: "What are you going to find out about in this book?"
- Ask the children what they know about wild cats. If you want to find out about a wild cat, which page would you look on?
- If you want to find out about a wild rat, which page would you look on?
- Look at page 10. Why do you think a wild rat would not make a good pet?
- Why do you think wild animals would not like to live with people?

## EXPLORING LANGUAGE

### Terminology
Title, cover, photographs, author, photographers

### Vocabulary
**Interest words:** hunts, tame, wild, burrows
**High-frequency words:** these, that, don't, them, take
**Positional word:** in

### Print Conventions
Capital letter for sentence beginnings, periods, commas